This special storybook belongs to:

, 08.

....

Snow & Ice withdrawn

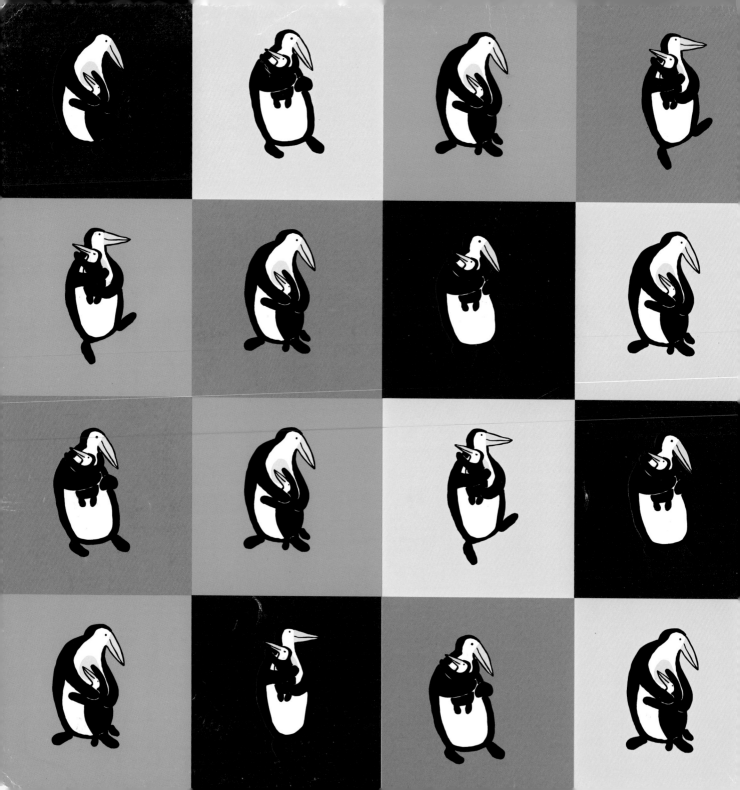

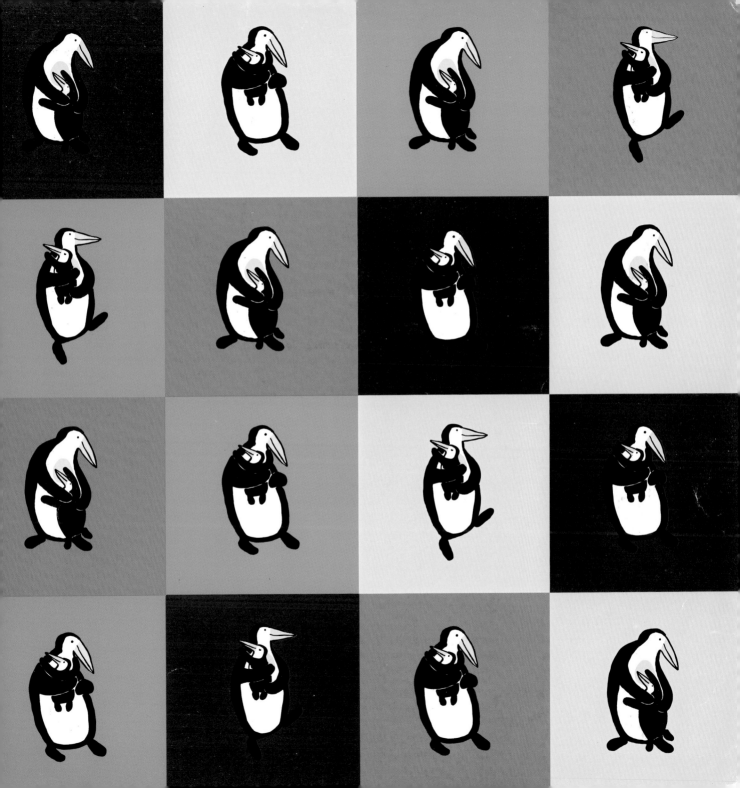

To Brian

First published in paperback in Great Britain 1997
This edition published in Great Britain 2001
by Egmont Books Limited
239 Kensington High Street
London W8 6SA

Copyright © Mary Murphy 1997
Mary Murphy has asserted her moral rights

ISBN 0 7497 4589 4

3 5 7 9 10 8 6 4 2

Printed and bound in Singapore

I like it

when

you

hold

my

hand

I like it

when

you

let

me

help

I like it when we

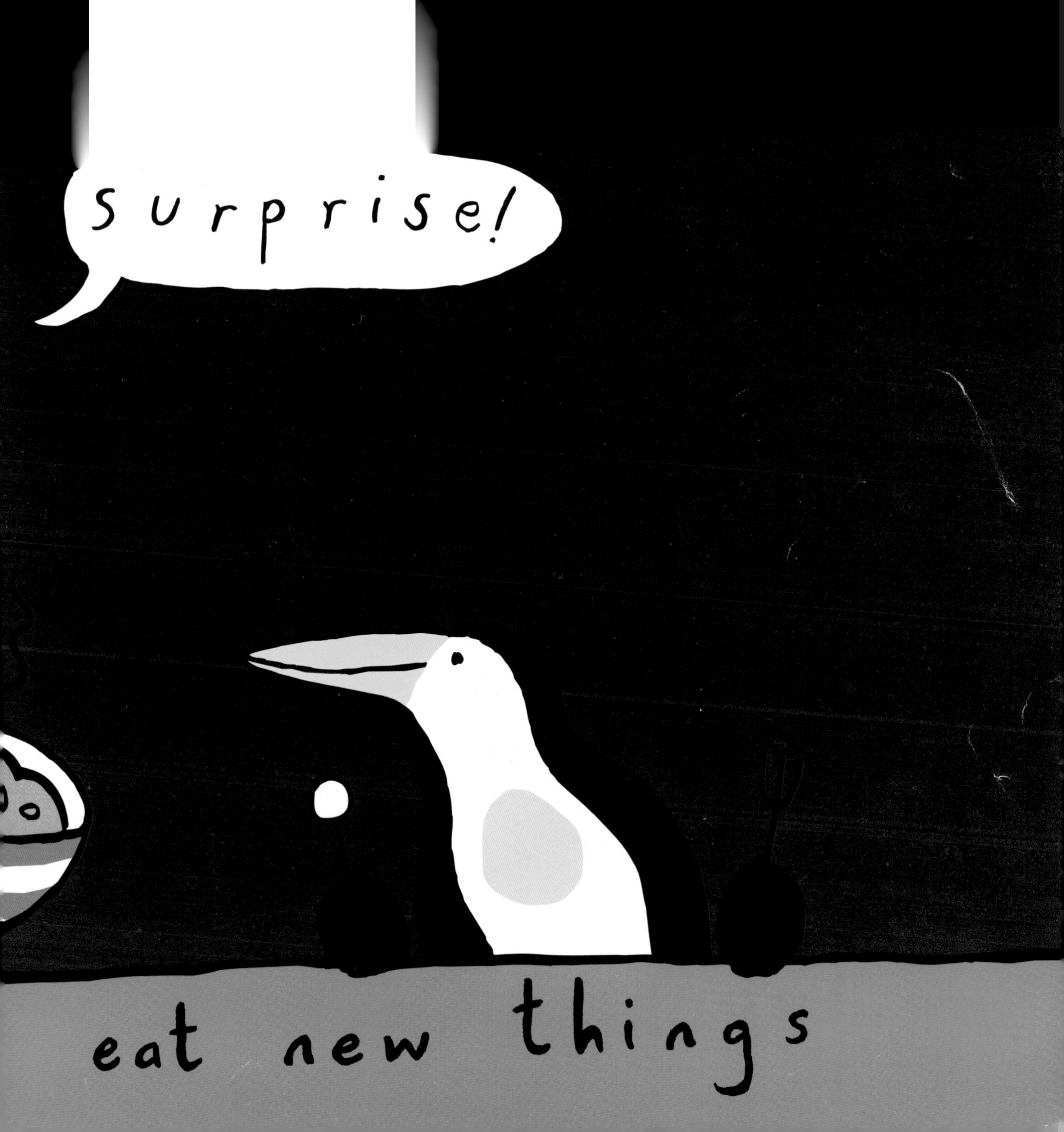
surprise!
eat new things

I like it when we

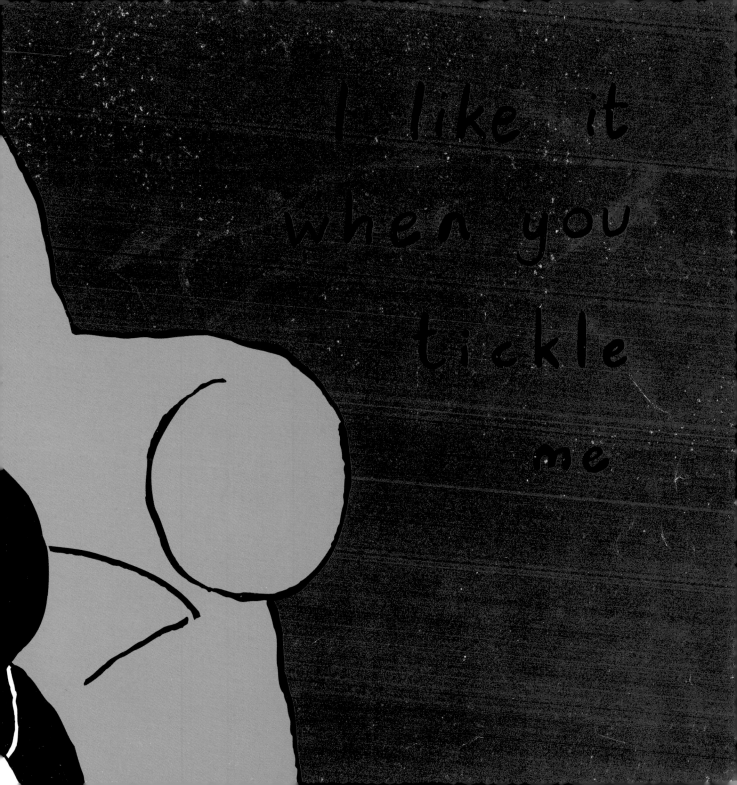

I like it when

I like it
when
you
read
me
stories

I like it when

you hug

I like it when we
splash about

I like it
when
we
kiss
goodnight

you're wonderful!

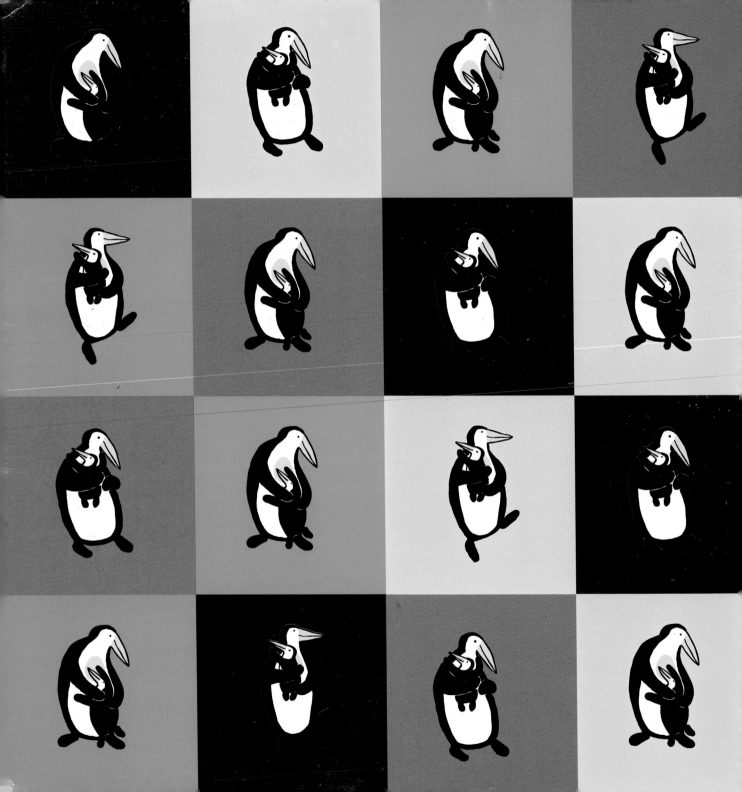

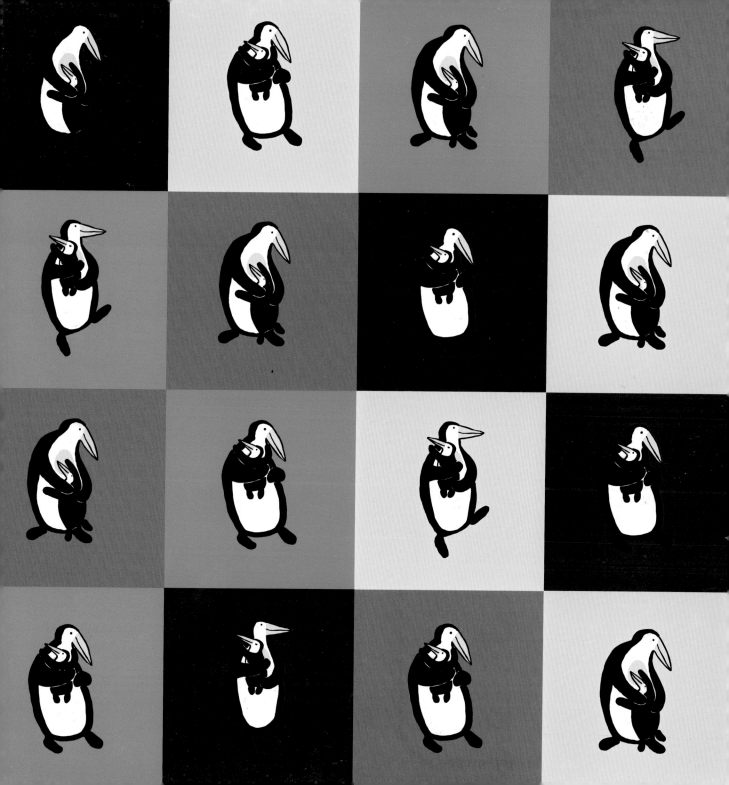

There are lots more Little Penguin stories
for you to enjoy: